Win or Lose

created by
Sharon M. Hart

written by
Sharon Dennis Wyeth

illustrated by
Sandy Rabinowitz

A
LITTLE APPLE
PAPERBACK

A Parachute Press Book

SCHOLASTIC INC.

New York Toronto London Auckland Sydney

For Georgia and her cousins—
Gina, Gary, Gregory,
Sheri, and Marc

Cover illustration by Rudy Nappe
No part of this publication may be reproduced in whole or in part, or
stored in a retrieval system, or transmitted in any form or by any
means, electronic, mechanical, photocopying, recording, or otherwise,
without written permission of the publisher.
For information regarding permission, write to Scholastic Inc.,
730 Broadway, New York, NY 10003.

ISBN 0-590-41504-2

12 11 10 9 8 7 6 5 4 3 2 1   9/8 0 1 2 3 4/9

Printed in the U.S.A.   11

First Scholastic printing, April 1989

Contents

Chapter One

---◆---

Arden's Dream Horse

"Look at her go!" Arden Quinn yelled. "Come on, Glory!"

Arden's heart pounded as Glory streaked by like black lightning. It was the filly's first practice run on the Wentworth track and Joey Ortega, Glory's trainer, was letting her show her speed. As they galloped around the turn and across the finish line, Arden craned her neck to see Mr. Wentworth's stopwatch.

"How was her time?" Arden cried.

"Excellent!" Wentworth replied. "She's a dream of a horse."

"Then can she run in the race?" Arden

asked. Her big, dark eyes fastened on her companion's sun-weathered face. Not only was Jed Wentworth the owner of Wentworth Track and Stables, one of the most successful stables in Florida — he was also Glory's owner. He was the only one who could decide whether the filly Arden loved so much would be allowed to run in the upcoming Wentworth Charity Race.

"Please, Mr. Wentworth," Arden begged. "You said that if Glory got strong enough, and Joey and I trained her right, and — "

The tall stable owner smiled broadly. "Don't worry, young lady, you've got your way! You and Joey Ortega were determined to get that filly ready for a real race and I'd be the last one to say you haven't done just that!"

"Hurray!" Arden shouted. She tore off to meet Joey and Glory as they trotted in around the back straightaway. "Mr. Wentworth says Glory can run in the race! He says her time is excellent!"

"She was feeling her oats, all right!" Joey called back as he brought Glory to a halt. The horse tossed her mane and gently nudged Arden's shoulder when the girl came over.

"You did real good, Glory!" Arden said, throwing her arms around the horse's neck. Arden's own thick ponytail almost matched the filly's dark, glistening mane. "I knew you could do it!" Arden whispered. "I knew you were a racer!"

Wentworth waved at them from the other side of the track. "Nice going!" he called to Joey. "Bring her in!"

"Why don't you take her?" Joey said, slipping down off the horse and motioning to Arden.

Arden smiled and hopped up into the saddle. "Giddyap, girl," she said softly, giving Glory a pat.

Ever since Arden's grandfather, Thomas Quinn, had bought Glory at an auction and saved her from the slaughterhouse, Arden had felt something very special for the filly. Not even Joey, who

3

used to be a jockey, or Arden's grand-mother, Tansy Quinn, who was a vet-erinarian, had Arden's "touch" with the horse. When Gramp brought Glory to the Quinns' animal rescue farm, River Oaks, the filly was nothing but skin and bones, and so skittish and ornery that no one thought she could ever be ridden. No one but Arden.

In time, Gran and Joey nursed Glory back to health, but it was Arden who gave her the special love she needed. When the time came for Glory to ride again, Arden was the only one who could manage her. It was Arden the filly first trusted. Of course, Arden hadn't known then that Glory really belonged to Went-worth, that she'd been stolen and then abused and abandoned by one of the stable owner's former employees.

And now, as Arden, Joey, and Glory reached the grandstand, Mr. Wentworth greeted them with a big grin. "You folks are miracle workers," he said. "For a while there, I didn't think Glory had much of a future — not after that bad beginning she had. I sure am glad she found her way to River Oaks."

Arden laid a gentle hand on Glory's head. It was pure luck that the horse had ended up on the animal rescue farm just a few weeks after Arden and her two brothers had come to spend a year with their grandparents in Florida. Arden's parents, Joanna and Walt Quinn, were halfway around the world in Africa on a yearlong photography expedition. At first Arden had missed them — and her home in Connecticut — terribly. But then Glory came along, and things fell right into place. The horse needed her so much, she hadn't had time to miss her parents.

What a great moment it had been when Mr. Wentworth announced that even though Glory was really his, he wouldn't be taking her back to Wentworth Stables right away! That he wanted to board her at River Oaks. . . .

Mr. Wentworth must have been sharing Arden's thoughts, for he suddenly looked at his stopwatch again and patted Glory proudly. "This filly's come a long way," he said. "Her mama, Midnight Clear, was a prizewinner. Maybe Glory will be one, too. We'll soon have the chance to find out — thanks to you, Arden!"

Arden blushed, but her dark eyes sparkled.

"So, how do we go about signing Glory up for the race?" Joey asked. "There is the matter of the entry fee."

"Entry fee?" gulped Arden. She'd been so eager for Glory to qualify, she hadn't thought to ask if it cost anything.

Wentworth waved his hand impatiently. "You should know better than that, Joey. I'll cover the entry fee for Glory."

The trainer nodded. "Just checking, sir. After all, it was Miss Quinn's idea to run Glory and I'm thinking that with her grandpa in the hospital and all — "

"I won't hear another word about

it," Wentworth interrupted. "Don't you think I'm glad to have Glory running in the race? After all, she may be your number-one boarder at River Oaks, but technically speaking she *is* still mine."

"Yes, sir — she's your horse, all right," said Joey.

"For the time being, at least," added Wentworth.

Arden gave the stable owner a worried look. One of her secret fears was that Wentworth would take Glory away from River Oaks and sell her. She and Glory spent so much time together — it really seemed as if Glory was *her* horse.

"So, what about the prize money?" Joey asked, leaning against the fence. "If Glory happens to place, who will that go to?"

"There'll be a thousand dollars for the owner and another thousand for the jockey," Wentworth said smoothly.

Arden looked over at Joey. The handsome young trainer seemed discontent. Arden knew he wasn't concerned for

7

himself. He was only looking out for her. But Arden didn't care about the money. It made her happy just knowing that Glory would get a chance to compete.

"Maybe I'm out of turn in speaking up," Joey said stubbornly, "but I think it's only fair that Miss Quinn — "

Wentworth looked amused. "Don't you worry about Arden. I'm not out to cheat anybody, especially her. Didn't I just say that I'm only Glory's owner for the time being?"

"You mean you've found a buyer for her?" Joey sputtered.

Arden spun around, startled. "You're not going to sell her!"

"Who said anything about selling her?" Wentworth said, his eyes twinkling. "But first things first. If Glory's running in the race, somebody's got to train her!"

"I can keep working with her," Joey offered.

"Thanks," Wentworth said. "I can't

think of a better man for the job. And I still want Glory boarding at River Oaks."

Arden gave a sigh of relief. No matter what happened after the race, at least she and Glory wouldn't be separated right away.

Wentworth rubbed his chin. "Now about the jockey," he continued.

"Who are you going to get?" asked Arden.

"I have a young rider in mind," Wentworth replied. "A girl. If anybody can handle Glory on the track, she can do it."

Arden came closer. "Who is she?"

"A good-looking girl," Wentworth said, "though she's a bit small for her age. I'm sure you know her. She's got big brown eyes and a long dark pony-tail."

Arden thought for a minute. The only girl she knew who rode horses was her neighbor, Tiffany Van Vreen. But Tiffany was tall and blonde. Arden herself was the only girl she could think of with a brown ponytail. But she knew *she* was too young to ride in the race.

Joey gave Jed Wentworth a grin. "Do I know this girl, too?" he asked.

Wentworth returned Joey's smile. "Oh, I think you do. Of course, I'll have to ask permission from her grandmother . . . Tansy Quinn."

"Wait a minute!" Arden exclaimed. "It *can't* be me!"

"Why not?" Mr. Wentworth said, laughing. "You're the best girl rider with a ponytail I know."

Arden blushed again. "But . . . I'm not old enough. According to the rules, all riders have to be between eleven and sixteen. And I'm only nine and a half."

"I already got the board to waive that rule for you," Wentworth explained. "I was hoping Glory would be able to run, and I figured you would be the best one to ride her."

Arden gasped. "Wow! Thanks, Mr. Wentworth! I'll work real hard with her!"

"I know you will," Wentworth said. "Of course, I'll still have to ask your grandmother — "

"It'll be okay with Mrs. Quinn," Joey broke in eagerly. "And I can be training Arden while I'm training Glory. She'll be a top-flight jockey by the time I get through with her!"

"Good!" Wentworth said, giving Glory a pat on the rump. "Now, how about getting this dream horse into the stable for a rubdown?"

Arden was in a daze as she helped Joey lead Glory into the stable. "Can you believe it, Joey? I was hoping Glory could be in the race, but I never dreamed I'd be riding her!"

Joey smiled. "I bet your brothers will be excited!"

"Yeah!" said Arden. "I can't wait to give Tim and Jesse the good news. And Gran and Gramp," she added quickly.

"Mr. Quinn will be pleased," said Joey. "That Jed Wentworth is really something — getting the board to let you ride! He told me he asked them to make an exception for you because you really are exceptional!''

Arden's voice echoed in the stable. "Did you hear what he said about Glory? He called her a dream horse!''

Minutes later Arden, Joey, and Glory were on their way home to River Oaks. The stable doors had barely closed behind them when a tall, blonde girl in immaculate riding clothes stepped out of the shadows. She'd been eavesdropping on their conversation from one of the other stalls.

"So little Miss Perfect and her dream horse are going to be in the race!'' the girl muttered. She watched Joey help Arden load Glory into the trailer. "Why is everybody so nice to that Arden Quinn?'' she hissed. "She makes me sick! I hate her!''

Chapter Two

Bad News

"Ti–im! Timmy!"

Tansy Quinn's voice carried over the meadow to where her eleven-year-old grandson sat astride a baby elephant.

"Coming, Gran!" Tim answered.

Slipping off the elephant's back, he tethered her beneath a shade tree. "Stay here, Thomasina. I'll be right back," the boy promised, as he ran over to his grandmother. He could tell she was on her way to the hospital — she was wearing her "dress-up" sun hat.

"Going to visit Gramp?" he asked, coming to a stop by the fence. The children's grandfather was in the hospital recovering from an appendicitis attack.

Gran nodded. "I thought I'd bring him the newspapers and some of those brownies Arden made last night."

"Don't forget our cards," Tim reminded her.

"I've got them right here in my satchel," she said. "Your grandfather's going to love the drawing of Thomasina."

Tim looked down at the ground. Although he prided himself on his ability to draw, compliments always embarrassed him. "I thought Gramp would get a kick out of it," he said. "He was sort of worried about Thomasina before he went into the hospital."

"How's our little girl doing?" Gran asked, peering out into the meadow. "Did she eat well?"

"Like an elephant!" Tim joked. "In fact, I'm going to leave her out for a little more grazing."

Tansy's blue eyes shone behind her glasses. "You kids are doing a good job around here. Your Gramp will be awfully proud of you."

"Tell him not to worry," Tim said. "Arden, Jesse, and I can handle everything."

"Not everything," Gran warned gently. "You know the lions and bears are off-limits."

"Sure," Tim said. "We never go into the enclosures without one of the keepers."

Gran tucked a stray hair up under her hat. "There's a cold supper for you in the refrigerator," she said. "I didn't leave anything on the stove this evening. It's too hot. See that your brother and sister get to bed at a reasonable hour. You, too," she added. "Don't let me catch you up when I get back."

"Yes, ma'am," Tim said.

Tansy started toward the jeep in the driveway, then looked back. "By the way, where's Jesse? I haven't seen him since lunchtime. I hope he and Pegleg aren't wandering around by the swamp."

"You sent him to the post office," Tim answered. "Remember?"

Gran pursed her lips. "Ummm . . . and what about Arden?"

Tim gave his grandmother a puzzled

glance. "Arden's at Wentworth Track and Stables," he reminded her. "With Joey. She told you good-bye after breakfast."

Gran shrugged and tapped herself on the forehead playfully. "Guess I'd forget my own head if it wasn't screwed on. Honestly, I've got so much on my mind these days."

Tim watched his grandmother climb into the jeep and go chugging down the driveway. He wished there were more he could do to help her. Tansy Quinn was the veterinarian at River Oaks, and with nearly two hundred animals she always had her hands full. Since Gramp's appendicitis she'd had to handle all the business and supervise the trainers, too. It was no wonder she seemed a little distracted.

Running River Oaks was too big a job for one person, Tim thought. He and Jesse and Arden did what they could around the house and in the stables, and Tim made it his business to keep his eye on things at the wildlife enclosures. But it just wasn't enough.

Tim took out a handkerchief and wiped his face and neck. Don't worry, Gran, he thought. We won't let you and Gramp down. . . .

Just then, Tim's younger brother, Jesse, came barreling along on his bicycle. As usual, he was accompanied by his three-legged dog, Pegleg.

"Tim!" Jesse cried. "We've got a postcard from Mom and Dad! It's from Nairobi!"

Tim swung over the fence and Jesse threw down his bicycle. "See?" Jesse said, waving the card. "This is the village where they stayed. They slept outside all night and — "

"Let me read it!" Tim said.

Jesse handed over the postcard and fanned himself with his cap. "Wow, it must be a hundred degrees today! If it's this hot in Florida, I wonder what it's like in Africa. Mom and Dad must be burning up!"

"They took a night expedition to photograph lions," Tim said, reading the card. "Sounds wild!"

"Yeah," Jesse agreed. "It must be neat sneaking up on the lions to take their pictures."

"Scary, too," said Tim. "Mom and Dad sure have lots of nerve."

"What's the matter, Pegleg?" Jesse said. The little dog had flopped down on the ground and was panting noisily.

"He's probably thirsty," said Tim. "Come to think of it, so am I. Oh, no!" he cried, looking across the meadow. "Where's Thomasina? She must have gotten loose!"

"There she is!" yelled Jesse. "Over by the stable!"

Tim sighed with relief when he spotted the elephant. "I guess we're not the only ones who got hot," he said. "When I left her, there was plenty of shade under that tree."

"Maybe she wants some water, too," said Jesse. The two boys started toward the stable with Pegleg hobbling after them. Jesse still had the rest of the mail in his hands.

"What else did the postman bring?" Tim asked.

"Nothing for us," his brother answered.

Tim put the postcard in his shirt pocket. "I'll show this to Arden when she gets back from Wentworth's."

Jesse ran a hand through his curly red hair. "I wonder if Mr. Wentworth is going to let Glory run in the race," he said. "Do you think she's fast enough?"

"Oh, Glory's fast enough, all right," said Tim. "I've been watching some of her training runs with Joey."

The boys stopped by the pump outside the stable. "Here you go, Pegleg," Jesse said, tossing the mail on the ground and grabbing the pump handle. A cool stream of water flowed out of the pump and into a puddle. Pegleg lapped at it greedily.

"Why don't you fill a bowl for him?"

Tim asked Jesse. "I'll get a bucket for Thomasina."

While Tim wandered off to get the bucket, Jesse filled an old tin bowl for Pegleg. Then he cupped his hands under the pump and took a long drink himself. "This is great!" he said, splashing his face. "I feel like putting my head under."

"Why don't you?" Tim said, coming back with a bucket and dipper. "But first move over and let me have some."

Tim got a dipperful of water for himself and then filled up the bucket.

"Is Thomasina all right?" Jesse asked.

"She'll be okay once she has some

water," Tim said, eyeing the elephant across the yard.

"Maybe we should hose her off," Jesse suggested. "That's what Arden does to Glory when she's hot."

"Good idea," said Tim. He picked up the bucket and started to walk away, then stopped and looked down at something on the ground. "What's this stuff?"

Jesse glanced over at his brother. "The rest of the mail," he answered sheepishly.

"What's the idea?" Tim exclaimed. "You put it where it could get all wet."

Jesse looked guilty. "Gosh," he said, bending down to examine the stack of envelopes. "It did get a little wet. But it'll dry off, won't it?" He picked up one of the envelopes and held it, dripping, upside down. It was so wet that the glue had come off and part of the wet letter was sticking out.

"Look at that!" Tim scolded. "Gran won't even be able to read it!"

Jesse pulled the letter out. "Let's put

it in the sun to dry!" he suggested.

"Don't you know it's a federal of-
fense to open other people's mail!" Tim
said, crossing over to grab the letter.
But as he was folding the letter to stick
it back into the envelope, his eye caught
the word *Warning!* "Oh, no!" he groaned,
quickly scanning the rest of the sentence.

Jesse came closer. "What's wrong?"

Tim pointed to the letter. "It's this!
It's from the bank!"

"What does it say?" Jesse asked.
"What's the matter?"

Tim didn't even look up. He knew
it was wrong to read other people's mail,
but it was right in front of his face!

"Come on!" Jesse said. "What does
it say?"

"Gran and Gramp are in big trouble,"
Tim finally replied. "They owe the bank
a lot of money for their mortgage on
River Oaks!"

"How much?" asked Jesse.

Tim gulped. "A lot," he repeated.
"Two thousand dollars!"

Chapter Three

Tiffany's Challenge

"Take it easy, now," Joey warned Arden. "This is a light day for Glory. I only want her to walk and canter — no galloping."

Arden nodded as she adjusted Glory's saddle. Tim's and Jesse's mounts were ready to go. Tim would be riding Gramp's horse, Ruby. Jesse would be on Ernie, a Shetland pony.

"Let Ruby set the pace," Joey told Tim. "Glory will follow along beside her."

"How come Ruby gets to be the leader?" Jesse asked, climbing onto his pony.

"Ruby's older and calmer," the trainer explained. "She'll keep the pace steady."

"I'm ready!" said Arden. She climbed up onto the filly and stroked her mane. "Come on, Glory."

Tim made a little noise with his tongue and Ruby moved out in front. Glory and Arden were not far behind, with Jesse and Ernie bringing up the rear. "Here, Pegleg!" Jesse called, looking over his shoulder. "Here, boy! We're going!"

"There he is," Joey said. "Over by the chickens! You, Pegleg! Come here!"

The little dog looked up and wagged his tail. When he saw Jesse, he tore across the yard and ducked under the fence rail. Soon all three Quinns, followed by the yipping dog, were headed across the meadow.

"Be back here in an hour!" Joey called after them. "And remember what I said about going fast!"

Arden waved. "Don't worry!" she yelled. "We'll take it easy!" She clucked

her tongue and Glory moved up next to
Ruby.

"Joey sure is strict about this training
business," Tim said.

"He has to be," Arden told him.
"Training a racehorse isn't easy. You
have to be real careful about what kind
of exercise they get."

"But doesn't Glory have to practice
galloping?" he asked.

"We'll do that at the track tomorrow," Arden explained. "Joey's going
to — "

"Look at Pegleg!" Jesse broke in. "He's trying to eat a butterfly!"

"If he can ever catch one!" laughed Arden. The little dog was hopping through the clover, stirring up swarms of insects. Every time a butterfly rose from the grass, he went after it with his mouth open.

"I hope the day of the race is as nice as today," Arden said. The brilliant blue sky was strewn with cottony white clouds, and a breeze blew through the lush green saw grass. Glory tossed her

silky mane and snorted with pleasure. She seemed content to be walking with Ruby.

"I can't believe how great it is down here," Arden said. "There used to be a lot of things about Florida I didn't like. But lately I don't even mind the mosquitoes."

"I always *liked* mosquitoes," Jesse bragged. "I know how to trap them. I can trap all kinds of things."

"Maybe you could catch some tarantulas," Arden teased. "Or we could ride by the swamp and you could catch a snapping turtle."

"Why not?" Jesse said, sticking his chin out. "As long as somebody holds Pegleg. Otherwise he might get into a fight with one of those turtles."

"We'll ride in the meadow," Tim instructed shortly.

Arden looked across at her big brother. His face was thoughtful. "Why don't we canter some?" she asked.

"Not yet," he said. "I wanted to ask

you something." Arden gave Tim a worried glance. He looked awfully serious all of a sudden.

"If you knew that somebody you cared about was in a lot of trouble — "

Arden wrinkled her nose. "Who? Who are you talking about?" she interrupted.

"*Somebody,*" Tim answered impatiently. "If this person didn't know about the trouble and you figured that — "

"I know who he's talking about!" Jesse chimed in.

"Let me tell her!" Tim snapped. But before Tim could say another word, Pegleg let out a sharp yelp.

"What's the matter?" Jesse exclaimed as the dog began whining and licking at his side.

"Maybe a yellow jacket got him!" Tim suggested.

"I hope it wasn't a snake!" Jesse said, jumping down from Ernie and running to his dog.

"What is it?" Tim asked, bringing

his horse to a halt. Arden and Glory pulled up beside them.

Suddenly Jesse grabbed at his head and cried, "Hey! What's the big idea? Somebody threw something at me!"

Arden and Tim quickly looked around. They were very close to Terrabella, the Van Vreen estate. The Quinns' snobbish neighbors separated their land from River Oaks with a gleaming white fence.

"Look!" shouted Tim. "That's who's throwing stuff! It's that kid, Tony!"

Sure enough, peeking out from behind a palmetto on the other side of the fence was the pudgy face of Tony Van Vreen. He was just about to hurl another round of baby oranges.

"What do you think you're doing?" Tim demanded. "You hit my brother in the head with one of those."

The little red-faced boy gave Tim a smirk. "Sorry. I didn't mean to get your brother. I was aiming for the dog."

"*You* hit Pegleg!" Jesse cried. "No

wonder he was howling! You could have hurt him!"

"So what?" said Tony. "He's already got one leg missing. I don't know why you want to keep a stupid-looking dog like that anyway!"

"He's not stupid!" Jesse yelled. "You're just jealous because your stupid aunt won't let you have a dog!"

Tony's beady eyes got smaller. "I wouldn't want a three-legged little mutt, anyway! When *I* get a dog, it's going to be a great big Doberman!"

Jesse got so mad he rushed over to the fence and began to climb over. Tony Van Vreen ran and hid behind a bush.

"Jesse!" Arden called. "Stop it! Come back here! You're going to get us in trouble!"

"But he hit Pegleg!" Jesse sputtered.

Arden rode over on Glory. "It's okay," she said. "Let's not cause any trouble. Mrs. Van Vreen will only complain."

"That's right," said Tim. "Gran's got enough on her mind right now. Let's just get out of here," he added, picking up Ruby's reins again.

"Wait a minute!" a voice called out.

Arden looked over the fence as a young blonde girl came riding up on a sleek brown colt. It was Tiffany Van Vreen. As usual she was dressed in a perfectly tailored set of riding clothes.

"Don't go anywhere, Arden Quinn," she commanded. "I want to talk to you."

"Leave me alone, Tiffany," Arden answered. "It was your little brother's fault. He was throwing oranges at Jesse's dog."

Tiffany trotted up to the fence. "That's not what I wanted to talk to you about," she said haughtily. "I hear you're riding Glory in the Wentworth race!"

"News sure travels fast," said Arden.

"I'm riding in the race, too!" the girl announced grandly. "Only I'll be riding my very own horse."

Arden flinched. Tiffany knew it was a sore spot that Glory didn't really belong to her.

"Too bad *you* don't have your own horse," Tiffany continued, rubbing it in. "My aunt just gave me a lot of money for my birthday so that I could buy a new one. Then I'll have two horses that belong to me!"

"Good for you," Arden said weakly. She was always overwhelmed by the

Van Vreens' vast wealth. "But even if I did have a horse all my own," she added in a stronger voice, "I'd still want to ride Glory."

Tiffany smiled sarcastically. "I think it's great that Mr. Wentworth's even letting Glory run in the race. I guess he feels sorry for her."

"Why should he feel sorry for Glory?" Tim asked hotly.

"Because the poor thing was in such wretched shape when your grandfather found her," Tiffany smirked.

"Glory's just fine now," Arden said, struggling to control her temper. "She's a beautiful horse."

Tiffany tossed her curls. "Just because she looks good doesn't mean she can compete in a race with real race-horses!"

"Glory's mother was a racehorse!" Arden shot back. "She was a winner!"

"And Glory's going to win, too!" said Tim.

"Don't make me laugh," Tiffany sneered.

"You're just jealous!" Jesse exploded. "You wish you had Glory for yourself!"

Tiffany's face turned bright red. Jesse had hit near the truth. Although Tiffany had shown nothing but scorn for Arden and Glory from the moment she'd met them, she'd recently had a change of heart — at least about the filly.

"Why would I want Glory when I already have Winsome?" Tiffany said, glaring at Arden's younger brother.

"Because Glory can run faster!" Jesse said.

"Oh, yeah?!" Tony said, climbing the fence to stick his tongue out at Glory.

"Don't you stick your tongue out at my sister's horse!" Jesse shouted. "Do it again and I'll punch you!"

Tim jumped off Ruby and grabbed Jesse by the arm. "Calm down," he said. "Don't pay any attention to him!"

"There's one way of settling this,"

Tiffany challenged. "Glory and Winsome could have a race right now — down to those palm trees at the end of the meadow."

Arden eyed Tiffany defiantly. There was nothing she'd have liked better than to show the snooty girl up. Sensing all the excitement, Glory was already pawing the ground.

"Do it, sis!" Jesse cried. "Glory could beat that wimpy horse without even trying!"

"Remember what Joey said," Tim warned. "No galloping."

"Tim's right," Arden agreed. "I can't run the risk of hurting Glory. Today's supposed to be one of her light days."

"Sounds to me like you're afraid Winsome will beat her," Tiffany gloated.

"You're just a chicken," Tony piped up.

"We'll see about that the day of the race," Arden shot back. "Come on Jesse and Tim — let's get out of here!" And with that, all three Quinns headed back across the field.

Jesse carried Pegleg up on the saddle until they were well away from Terrabella. "I don't understand that Tony Van Vreen," he muttered. "How could he be so mean to Pegleg? He must really hate animals."

"Just like his aunt," Tim said. "I don't think she even likes horses. She probably only keeps them around for show. She thinks Gran and Gramp are a menace for running an animal rescue farm."

"Those stupid Van Vreens," Jesse added. "I bet they'd be really glad if River Oaks did have to close down."

"What are you talking about?" Arden asked. "Who said anything about closing the farm?"

Tim sighed. "That's what I was trying to tell you before," he explained. "The people I care about who are in trouble are Gran and Gramp. I accidentally saw a letter from the bank, and it said that they owe two thousand dollars."

"Two thousand dollars!" Arden gasped. "How are they ever going to get that much money?"

"I don't know," Tim said quietly. "Jesse and I . . . well, we haven't told Gran yet. We were afraid it might upset her."

"But what will happen if Gran and Gramp can't pay the money?" Arden was alarmed.

Tim looked very upset. "What do you think?"

In spite of the heat, Arden shivered. If the bank shut down River Oaks, it would be the end of the world for her grandparents and all the animals they had rescued. It would be the end of everything!

Chapter Four

Tim's Plan

"We've got to write to Mom and Dad!" said Tim. "They'll know what to do."

"But they're in Nairobi," Arden moaned. "It takes a long time for mail to get there."

Jesse plopped down on the bed with his legs dangling over the side. Pegleg pounced on one of his sneakers.

"Why don't we just show Gran the letter?" Jesse asked, wrestling the dog with his foot. "Gran and Gramp are rich, aren't they?"

"They have a lot of property," Tim answered, "but that doesn't mean they have a lot of money."

Arden nodded. "I heard Mom and Dad say that Gran and Gramp were in over their heads, because they can't stand to turn away an animal."

"The only thing to do is write that letter," Tim said, tearing a piece of paper out of his sketchbook.

Jesse sat up. "What about a telegram?"

"Now you're thinking!" Tim said. "I can take it to the telegraph office this afternoon on my bike."

Tim sat down at his desk and began composing a message.

"How's this?" he asked after a few moments of silence.

" 'Mom and Dad: River Oaks in big trouble. Send two thousand dollars as soon as possible. Love, Tim, Arden, and Jesse.' "

Arden wrung her hands. "I just hope it gets there in time — and that Mom and Dad *have* two thousand dollars."

"They're getting paid a lot of money for their photography expedition," Tim assured her.

Jesse picked up Pegleg and began

pacing around the room. "If Mom and Dad don't send the two thousand dollars, maybe we could make it ourselves."

"How?" said Tim. "This isn't play money we're talking about."

"I could open up a lemonade stand," Jesse said hopefully. "Lots of people come into the visitors' park on weekends."

Tim shook his head. "I've heard that one before. The last time you sold lemonade it took you a month just to make six dollars."

"There *is* another way," Arden said.

Tim turned around to face her. "Let's hear it!"

"The Wentworth Charity Race," Arden said. "There's a prize for the first-place rider."

"I thought all the money was going to the children's hospital," Tim said.

"Most of it is," Arden explained, "but there are prizes for the owner *and* the rider of the winning horse. They each get a thousand dollars."

"A thousand dollars!" exclaimed Tim.

"Joey thinks Glory has a good chance of winning," Arden continued excitedly. "If she does, Mr. Wentworth will get a thousand dollars — and so will I! Then all we'd need — "

A light knock on the door interrupted Arden's words. She and her brothers turned to see their grandmother in the doorway. "Who wants to go with me to pick up the new camels?" Gran said.

"What camels?" Tim asked, snatching up the message to his parents and stuffing it into his pocket.

"The ones your grandfather promised to take in before he went to the hospital," Gran replied.

"But how *can* we?" Tim blurted out. "I mean . . . can we afford them?"

"Since when have you become a businessman?" Tansy Quinn smiled.

"But it must cost a lot of money to feed a camel," Tim answered.

"Always room for one more. Besides, your Gramp gave his word. Now, how about it? Who wants to come along?"

Tim gave Arden and Jesse a look. "Not me," he said. "I've got to go get some batteries for my flashlight."

"*I'll* go with you, Gran!" said Jesse.

"Me, too," Arden echoed.

Tansy Quinn smiled at them. "Good! I'll meet you outside. I just have to find my keys to the big trailer."

Arden and Jesse went downstairs to wait in the garden. Tim was just getting on his bicycle when a black sedan turned into the driveway.

"Beg your pardon," a tall, thin man said, stepping out of the car. "Is this the Quinn residence? I'd like to speak with Mr. Quinn."

Tim stepped forward. "I'm Timothy Quinn," he said. "My grandfather's not here now."

"I see." The man smiled and then reached into his pocket. "Will you leave this for him?" he said, pulling out a business card. "I'll call again, when he's at home."

Tim looked down at the card. *SOUTHLAND REALTY* was printed in big, bold letters, and underneath that in smaller type, *James Lucas*.

"Real estate. . . ." Tim mumbled. "I don't think my grandfather is interested in buying any land. River Oaks is pretty big."

"I know exactly how big River Oaks is," the man said. "Just give your grandfather my card, okay?"

Mr. Lucas was just getting back into his car when Gran came out of the house and walked briskly over. "I'm Tansy Quinn," she said. "May I help you?"

The real-estate man gave Gran a big smile. "We have clients who are looking for property in this area, ma'am. Before you put River Oaks on the market, my company would like you to give us a call."

Gran put on her glasses to study the card he gave her. "You're not the first developer to take an interest in River Oaks," she said pleasantly. "But Mr.

Quinn and I have no plans for putting our place on the market."

The man bowed and got back into his car. "I understand, Mrs. Quinn. These kinds of decisions take time. When you do make up your mind, just call me. Don't worry, my company will give you a good deal."

Gran shrugged as the black sedan headed down the driveway. "Where in the world did he get the idea we wanted to sell River Oaks?" she murmured to herself. Turning to Jesse and Arden, she said, "Come on, kids. The animal trailer's over at the stable."

Jesse and Pegleg followed Gran down the hill, while Arden lagged behind with Tim.

"That real-estate man must have found out about the debt," Tim whispered. "He knows if Gran and Gramp don't pay, they'll have to sell. Mom and Dad have got to help us!"

Arden drew a deep breath. "Or Glory and I have got to win that race!"

Chapter Five

Trouble at the Track

Tiffany Van Vreen sat in the grandstand, looking down at several young riders who were exercising their horses on the Wentworth track.

"None of them is as good as Winsome," she said smugly.

"Don't count your chickens," said Vince Shago, the Van Vreen's head trainer.

"Winsome's never been in better shape," Tiffany boasted. "If he won that race up north last month, why shouldn't he win this one?"

Vince rubbed his chin. "Things have a way of changing from race to race," he said, casting a quick glance back at the track. Arden and Glory were just trotting onto the turf, with Joey and Ruby right behind them.

Vince nudged Tiffany. "Check it out. There's your competition."

Tiffany followed Vince's gaze and her lips twisted into a pout. Arden Quinn again on that nag Glory! "Why is everybody always making such a fuss over that horse?" Tiffany snarled.

Vince shrugged. "Glory was an abused animal. Wentworth's impressed with the horse's comeback. And you've got to hand it to Arden. She pretty much brought that filly back to life single-handedly."

Tiffany's blue eyes glinted with spite. "Big deal," she muttered as an imposing-looking man in a derby hat sat down a few yards away.

"Look!" Tiffany pointed. "Isn't that Sam Silver?"

Vince nodded. "He must be looking to buy some new horses."

"Well, the only horse worth looking

at is Winsome," Tiffany said, "and he's not for sale!"

Vince kept his mouth shut — there was no point in arguing — but his eyes automatically shifted back to the track.

Glory appeared to be in fine form and Arden was clearly in excellent spirits.

"Easy does it, Arden," Vince heard Joey say. He was still riding alongside on Ruby. "Let her know who's boss."

Keeping a firm grip on the reins, Arden led Glory into a gallop.

"When you reach the turn," Joey coached, "take it a little faster."

Arden hugged the horse's flanks with her knees and urged the filly to a greater speed.

"That's it!" Joey called out just behind her. "You're looking good."

Joey and Arden slowed their horses down to a trot as they passed the grandstand. When she saw Tiffany and Vince, Arden waved politely.

Tiffany didn't wave back, but Vince

did. And the man in the derby tipped his hat.

"Who's that?" Arden asked Joey.

"Sam Silver," Joey said. "He's a big horse breeder from Kentucky."

Arden looked back over her shoulder. The man in the derby was busily puffing on a cigar, but his eyes were still on them. . . .

By the time Joey and Arden brought their horses in, Tiffany and Vince were in the ring with Winsome. "Nice going," Vince called out kindly.

"Thanks!" Arden answered. "It was a good day." Arden ignored the spiteful look on Tiffany's face. She rode back to the stable.

There, standing next to the fence, was Sam Silver, the man in the derby. It was almost as if he'd been waiting for them.

Mr. Silver offered his hand to Joey and turned to Arden and Glory. "Fine-looking filly," he drawled in a low, rumbling voice.

"Thanks," said Arden. "Her full name is Rappadan Glory. She belongs to Mr. Wentworth."

"Yes, I know," Silver said. He took another puff of his big cigar and put a hand out to Glory. The horse snorted and took a step backward.

"I guess she doesn't like cigar smoke," Joey said, stroking Glory's neck. "She's a real lady."

Mr. Silver cracked a smile and backed off politely. "She's a lady, all right," he agreed, "just like her mother."

"You know Glory's mother?" Arden asked eagerly.

"Well, sure," said Mr. Silver. "A few years back everybody knew Midnight Clear."

Just then Jed Wentworth came out of his office, and Mr. Silver waved at him in the distance. "Ho, Wentworth!" he commanded loudly. "I want to talk to you!"

Arden watched the man from Kentucky stride across the yard. He was even bigger and taller than Mr. Wentworth.

"Do you know Mr. Silver?" Arden asked Joey as they hoisted the saddles off Glory and Ruby.

"Only by reputation," Joey replied. "He's got plenty of horses and plenty of money to buy more with."

"Why does he want so many?" she asked curiously.

Joey shrugged. "Who knows? I guess he's always on the lookout for the perfect one — his dream horse."

"Dream horse!" Arden cried in alarm. "That's what Mr. Wentworth called Glory!"

"Now, don't you go searching for things to worry about," Joey said gently. "Just because Silver showed a little interest in Glory doesn't mean he wants to buy her."

"I hope not," Arden said. She put a protective arm around the filly's neck. But Mr. Silver had seemed more than just interested in Glory. And now he was deep in conversation with Mr. Wentworth. I wonder what they're talking about! Arden thought, glancing over her shoulder. Oh, please don't let it be about selling Glory!

The next time Arden and Joey came to practice at the track, Mr. Silver was nowhere in sight — much to Arden's relief. But Tiffany was there again. And this time it was Arden's turn to check out the competition.

"Isn't that Winsome up there?" Arden asked, looking toward the track.

Joey shaded his eyes to see better. "That's him, all right," he said.

Arden whistled as the brown colt sprinted up the straightaway. "Wow! He's fast!"

"Winsome's a good horse," Joey admitted, "but I don't think Miss Van Vreen is a very good rider."

"Why not?" asked Arden curiously. "She looks pretty good to me."

Joey shook his head. "She uses her whip too much."

Arden watched Winsome circle the track before turning away to groom Glory. Minutes later Tiffany came galloping down the hill on Winsome. While

Joey went over to talk to Vince, Arden finished getting Glory ready. She was just tightening the girth on Glory's saddle when Tiffany and Winsome pulled up beside her.

"Did you see Winsome out there?" Tiffany gloated.

"I saw," Arden answered. "He looked good."

Tiffany tossed her head. "Is that all you can say?" she demanded, as she got off the colt. She threw her riding crop and helmet onto the ground and sauntered over to the pump. "Winsome's favored to win this race!" she taunted.

"Mr. Wentworth says Glory has a good chance, too," Arden called back evenly.

"That's what you think!" Tiffany sneered. She walked over to Arden. As Arden stared into the girl's eyes, she suddenly had the feeling that Tiffany really hated her! It was hard for Arden to understand. She'd never had an enemy before.

"By the way," Tiffany said, looking down at the ground slyly, "Mr. Wentworth was looking for you earlier. He wants to see you in his office."

"Thanks," Arden mumbled, turning away. "Be back in a minute, Joey!" she called before running off toward the office.

Joey and Vince were still talking over by the paddock. So there was no one watching Tiffany as she took a furtive look around and then crept up next to Glory. . . .

By the time Arden came back from the office a few minutes later, Tiffany was standing just inside the stable with Winsome.

"Mr. Wentworth wasn't there," Arden said. "Do you know what he wanted?"

"How should I know?" the blonde girl answered rudely.

Arden shrugged and walked back over to Glory. "Ready, Joey!" she called brightly.

While Arden led the filly away from the stable and up the hill, Joey broke off his conversation with Vince Shago and took a seat in the bleachers. "I'll watch from here!" he called out.

Arden climbed onto Glory's back and took the reins. Following Joey's instructions, she eased the horse from a trot into a gallop.

The filly was still getting used to the track, but it was clear she loved running. "That's it, beauty!" Arden whispered, feeling Glory's pent-up power. "Let's see if you can go a little faster!"

As they approached the turn, the horse seemed to have wings. Arden's heart raced, too — she knew this was going to be a good run! But suddenly the saddle began to slip. Panic filled Arden's body. The horse was going so fast! How could she stop it?

Arden clung to Glory's neck for balance. "Hold on girl!" she gasped, struggling to slow the filly down. "Hold on! I'm falling. . . . "

Chapter Six

A Close Call

"Miss Arden! Miss Arden! What happened?" Joey rushed to Arden's side as Glory brought her in safely.

"It's the saddle, I think," Arden said breathlessly. "It's falling off. If it hadn't been for Glory. . . ."

Joey stroked the filly. "Good girl. You slowed up on your own, did you?"

"It was as if she *knew* I was in trouble," Arden explained, sliding down off the horse. "She didn't want to throw me."

Arden sighed with relief as her feet touched the ground. "That was a close call," she said. "I don't know what happened."

"The girth's loose," said Joey, inspecting the saddle. "Look at this."

Arden followed Joey's pointing finger. "It's on the last notch!" she exclaimed in surprise. "How did that happen?"

"Didn't you saddle Glory yourself?" Joey asked.

Arden nodded.

"Well, don't be in such a hurry next time," he warned. "This kind of carelessness can be dangerous."

"But I wasn't careless," Arden said. "I mean . . . I've never done that before."

"Maybe you're just tired," Joey said. "The best of us can overlook things when we need rest."

"But I'm not tired," said Arden.

"Then you must not have been concentrating when you tightened the saddle," Joey insisted.

"I *was* kind of talking to Tiffany," Arden admitted. It never occurred to her that the other girl might have had something to do with the loose saddle!

"Anyway," Joey added in a gentler tone, "you're not hurt. That's the important thing."

Arden leaned up against Glory and gave her a hug. "I guess," she said. "But I'm afraid we did lose some seconds off our time."

"Let's put the stopwatch away until tomorrow," Joey suggested. "Time to get home for supper."

"But we've got so much work to do!" Arden argued. "We've got to get better if we're going to win!"

"I'm the trainer," Joey said firmly, "and I don't want you pushing yourself — or your horse. Relax. There's always tomorrow."

Arden reluctantly agreed to call it a day.

"Bye-bye, Arden!" Tiffany called

gleefully. Arden waved, hardly noticing how cheerful Tiffany seemed all of a sudden.

All the way home in the trailer, Arden kept thinking about the loose saddle. How could I have been so dumb? she thought. Thanks to her, Glory had lost a whole afternoon of training!

Joey drove them back to River Oaks and dropped Arden off at the house.

"Hi, Arden!" Jesse yelled from the steps.

Arden turned and waved at her brother. Jesse had Mortie, the talking mynah bird, perched on his shoulder. Next to Pegleg, Mortie was Jesse's favorite animal companion.

"Hi, Jesse," Arden called. "Hi, Mortie."

"Have a Miner's Pretzel, please!" the bird squawked.

Arden couldn't help smiling. "Aren't you ever going to get tired of saying that, Mortie?" she asked, ruffling the bird's feathers.

"Not as long as we've got some of these left!" Jesse said, dipping his hand into a big sack on the ground marked *Miner's Pretzels*.

The bird hopped down to get one. "Miner's are finer!" he croaked loudly.

Arden and Jesse laughed. Earlier that month, Gramp had read in the newspaper that Miner's Pretzel Company was looking for a talking bird to do a television commercial. Gramp had trained

Mortie so well that the mynah bird had gotten the job. Too well, Gran complained — for now, weeks after Mortie's commercial, the bird was still repeating his lines over and over.

"When do you think we'll get to see Mortie's commercial on TV?" Jesse asked Arden.

Arden shrugged and popped a pretzel into her mouth. "We don't even need to. He does it right here for us every day, anyway. I wonder if he made any money from it," she added thoughtfully.

"Probably not," said Jesse. "I think they paid him in pretzels."

Arden sighed. If only they could think of other ways to raise money for River Oaks! After the mishap at the track that afternoon, she wasn't as confident about winning the thousand dollars.

"Any mail from Mom and Dad?" she asked Jesse hopefully.

"Not today."

"They must have gotten our telegram by now," Arden said. "Why haven't they answered?" She sighed as Tim came striding up the hill.

Tim's hair was sticking out all over. He was covered with straw and was carrying a wriggling little dog.

"There you are, Pegleg!" Jesse cried. "Where did you find him, Tim?"

"Down with the new camels," Tim answered, as Pegleg sprang out of his arms. "He's lucky he didn't get trampled by one of them."

Tim flopped down on the steps next to Arden. "How was Glory's time today?"

"We lost some seconds," Arden said quietly. "I didn't have the saddle on tight enough. I almost fell off."

"Not you!" Tim teased. "Not our own little Annie Oakley!"

"This is serious!" Arden protested. "Suppose I make a mistake like that on the day of the race? We have to get that prize money to save River Oaks!"

"We'll get it," Tim said. "Just because you had one bad run, that doesn't mean Glory can't win. Anyway, we should be hearing from Mom and Dad any day now."

"I hope so," said Arden.

"Maybe we should just tell Gran and Gramp," Jesse said.

"Not until we've tried everything!" Tim sounded determined. "Gran told me that Gramp just came down with the flu. That means he'll have to stay in the hospital even longer than we thought."

"He's going to be okay, isn't he?" Jesse asked with a worried frown.

"Sure," Tim replied. "Gran says it's not too serious. But it *does* mean we can't tell her about the letter from the bank! She's worried enough already!"

"That's right," Arden agreed. "We'll have to save River Oaks ourselves!"

Chapter Seven

In the Starting Gate

Tiffany climbed out of the Terrabella trailer and peered up at the track. It was so early in the morning, she'd expected to be the first rider at Wentworth's. But there was Arden already out exercising Glory while Joey watched from the side-line.

"Of all things!" Tiffany muttered with a scowl. "The one day *we* get here early to practice, *they* have to be here hogging the track!"

"I guess Arden and Joey got the jump on us," Vince Shago said cheerfully. He led Winsome down the ramp. "But don't worry. By the time we're ready, they'll probably be finished and the track will be free."

"I don't see why we have to wait," Tiffany grumbled, glaring in Arden's direction. "I should take Winsome out there right now. Then Arden Quinn would see what she's up against."

"I wouldn't suggest that," warned Vince. "Winsome and Glory aren't familiar with each other. It wouldn't be good for them to ride in company."

"It wouldn't be good for Glory, you mean," Tiffany said snidely. "If Glory and Winsome were running together, Winsome would show Glory up."

"Why don't you get Winsome ready for his warm-up?" Vince said, changing the subject. "I've got to go see Mr. Wentworth for a minute."

Tiffany took the grooming brush out of Vince's hand and flounced over to her horse. Even as she brushed the colt's shiny coat, she kept glancing up at Glory and Arden.

Meanwhile, out on the track, all of Arden's attention was focused on Joey.

"When you get to the homestretch," he said, "give the horse her head. Keep contact, but relax on the reins."

"Okay!" Arden replied, trotting off down the track. Following Joey's instructions to the letter, she leaned forward and urged the horse on. And when they reached the homestretch, she let Glory surge across the finish.

"That was great!" yelled Joey, looking at his watch. "Best yet!"

Arden slowed Glory up and cantered back. "It felt incredible!" she said. "Like we were flying!"

"It looked that way, too," Joey said, reaching into his pocket and giving Glory a carrot. "Good girl!" he said warmly. "That goes for both of you!"

Arden grinned and wiped her face with her handkerchief. She was so hot, her bangs were almost plastered to her forehead.

"Just one more lesson," Joey said,

"and then we're through for the morning. Since the gate is on the track today, I want you to practice starting."

"Sure thing," said Arden, following Joey toward the chute.

"See if you can keep her nice and quiet until I give the signal," Joey said. "And keep her nose up. She has to get used to waiting in position for the start of the race."

Just then Tiffany galloped up on Winsome. The girl's eyes were flashing with impatience. "Winsome has to practice starting, too!" she said.

"We'll be finished in a minute, miss," Joey said.

"You people act like you own the track," Tiffany huffed, throwing Arden a dirty look.

"Sorry," said Arden, trying to be polite. "We're almost through."

As soon as Glory was in the chute, the horse became restless. "Calm down, girl," Arden crooned. "We have to wait for the signal. This is how it will be the day of the race."

"Stay clear, Miss Van Vreen," Joey warned Tiffany as he got ready to operate the gate. "Are you sure you don't want to go down the hill? The bell may spook your horse."

"That won't happen," Tiffany said sharply. "Winsome and I will wait our turn, don't worry."

For just a moment Tiffany waited beside the gate, well away from Arden. But, when no one was looking, she began inching Winsome forward.

When Joey pulled the lever, Arden and Glory charged out on the inside position along the rail. At that instant, Tiffany and Winsome lunged down the middle of the track.

"Hey!" Joey exclaimed. Shading his eyes, he squinted after the horses as they galloped off into the distance. "What's that Van Vreen brat up to now?" he muttered.

Close to the inside rail, Arden was in the lead! She had been absolutely stunned when Tiffany started with her, but she was determined to give the girl a run for her money. She could almost feel Tiffany breathing down her neck.

"Come on, Winsome!" Tiffany commanded harshly. As they approached the first turn, the two horses were neck and neck. "Get out of my way!" Tiffany snarled at Arden. Edging in on Glory, she tried to bump her.

"What are you doing?" Arden cried in a panic. If Tiffany continued to crowd her, Glory might be pushed into the rail. "Move over!"

But Tiffany refused to yield. As Glory pulled ahead by a hair's-breadth, the blonde girl flailed at Winsome with her whip. "Come on!" she muttered through clenched teeth. "Let's get 'em!"

At the second turn, Tiffany veered sharply toward the inside in a final attempt to cut Arden off. Sensing the danger to herself and Glory, Arden gave the filly her head. The horse leaped forward and out of the way!

An instant later, Arden heard an angry scream, followed by a shrill whinny. She gradually brought Glory to a halt, then looked back over her shoulder. There was Tiffany, sitting on the ground with a scowl on her face, while Winsome ran loose on the track. The girl's colt had stumbled and thrown her!

The next morning, Gran, Arden, and Joey met in Mr. Wentworth's office along with Tiffany, Vince, and Tiffany's aunt, Mrs. Van Vreen. Having heard about the incident on the track the day before, the stable owner had called them all together.

As soon as everyone was seated, Jed Wentworth got straight to the point. "I have always prided myself on keeping a clean track," he began sternly. "I've kicked many a jockey or trainer off this place for misconduct. I would hate to think that one of you girls is guilty of unsportsmanlike behavior. . . . ''

Crossing behind his desk, Wentworth gave the two young riders a hard stare. Arden cringed. *She* knew she hadn't done anything wrong, but Mr. Wentworth was looking at her as if she were a total stranger.

"Yesterday there was nearly a serious accident on my track," Wentworth continued. "I want to know exactly what happened out there."

"I'll tell you what happened!" Mrs. Van Vreen squawked. The skinny, birdlike woman put an arm around Tiffany's shoulder. "That girl" — she pointed an accusing finger at Arden — "that vicious girl tried to injure my poor little niece!"

Arden's mouth flew open. "That isn't true!" she gasped.

"It is, too!" Tiffany whined. "You pushed Winsome and me out of the way!"

Arden's face went white with disbelief. She couldn't believe what a liar

Tiffany was. "We didn't push you," she choked. "You pushed us."

"I see we have a difference of opinion," Mr. Wentworth broke in. Raising an eyebrow, he turned to Joey. "Did you see what happened?"

"I was still back at the gate," Joey answered. "They were too far away for me to see what was really going on. But I do know that Miss Quinn would never do anything to deliberately hurt another rider!"

"Then why did Winsome stumble?" Mrs. Van Vreen demanded sharply. "Who's responsible for Tiffany being thrown?"

"Arden is!" Tiffany whimpered. "She was mad because Winsome and I were gaining on her. She tried to push me over at the turn on purpose."

"That isn't what happened!" Arden protested with a beseeching glance at Mr. Wentworth. He had to believe her!

"It's all right, Arden," Tansy Quinn whispered, placing a gentle hand on her granddaughter's shoulder. "Just tell Mr. Wentworth the truth."

"Glory and I were starting at the gate," Arden explained in a stronger voice. "Tiffany came onto the track, too. And when we got to the second turn, she tried to cut me off. I thought Glory was going to be pushed into the rail. We just jumped ahead — that's all. We had to!"

Wentworth rubbed his chin. "That would have been when Winsome stumbled," he said quietly.

"You're not taking *her* word over Tiffany's!" Mrs. Van Vreen exclaimed.

"I didn't say that, ma'am," Mr. Wentworth replied coolly.

"I should hope not!" Mrs. Van Vreen cried. "Besides, how can you judge things fairly when you're the owner of the horse that Arden was riding?!"

Wentworth's face reddened. "I'll have you know," he growled, "that I would disqualify one of my own jockeys for

misconduct before I'd disqualify anyone else."

Arden felt her throat tighten and her knees go wobbly. Surely Mr. Wentworth wasn't going to disqualify her!

Wentworth stood up from his desk. "I'm going to let you girls off with a warning," he said in a firm voice. "*This time*," he added. "But I want you to stay out of each other's hair from now on. If I hear of any more unfair behavior from either of you, I won't be so lenient. In my book, deliberately cutting off another rider is cheating, and I won't have cheating here at Wentworth."

"Yes, sir," Tiffany said primly.

"Yes, sir," Arden added in a shaky voice. Jumping up from her chair, Arden tore across the room and out the door.

"Wait, Arden!" she heard Gran call behind her.

But Arden couldn't face anyone just then — not even Gran. She ran past the cars and trailers parked in the yard and threw herself on the ground beneath a clump of palm trees. Then she covered her face with her hands and began to sob.

"I know how you feel, Arden," a soft voice said.

Arden sniffed and looked up. Her grandmother and Joey were looking at her sympathetically.

"It hurts when somebody accuses you of something you didn't do," Gran's soothing voice went on.

Arden threw herself into her grandmother's arms. "Oh, Gran!" she cried. "You don't think I tried to make Tiffany fall, do you? *You* don't think I'm a cheat!"

"Of course we don't!" Joey chimed in. "And neither does Jed Wentworth. We all know you better than that. You could never do anything dishonest."

Arden blinked back her tears. "I don't think I could," she said softly.

"Of course you couldn't," Gran said, getting up off the ground and giving Arden a hand. "You're Arden Quinn!

You've got too much of that Quinn honor to ever cheat at anything.''

Arden wiped her eyes and smiled at Gran and Joey. "Thanks . . . for believing me.''

"Why don't we take a vacation from the track for a day,'' Gran said, catching Arden by the hand. "How about a trip to the ice-cream parlor?''

"Good thinking, Mrs. Quinn,'' Joey said, fanning himself with his cap. "I could sure go for a butterscotch sundae. What about you, Arden?''

Arden grinned sheepishly. "I guess a big banana split might make me feel a little better.''

"I have some news that will make you feel a lot better,'' Gran said as they walked toward the car.

"What's that?'' Arden asked, squeezing her grandmother's hand.

"Your gramp is coming home tomorrow!''

Chapter Eight

———◆———

The Unwelcome Visitor

"They're here! They're here!" shouted Jesse from the back porch.

Tim and Arden were out in the meadow with Glory and Thomasina. Leaving the horse and elephant to graze, they tore back to the house just as Gran's jeep came bumping down the driveway.

"Gramp! Gramp!" they all yelled. "You're home!"

The minute Thomas Quinn got out of the jeep, Arden threw herself into his arms. Tim hugged him around the waist and Jesse pulled at his elbow. "Hey there, you little monkeys!" Gramp greeted them, hoisting Jesse up like a sack of potatoes.

"No roughhousing!" Gran scolded. "You'll tear your stitches."

"Don't you worry," said Gramp. "I

can still lift this peanut!" He shook Jesse playfully.

"Put me down, Gramp!" Jesse giggled.

Gramp put his grandson down and beamed at all three of the children. "I want to hear all the latest news," he said.

"Thomasina's doing great," Tim reported. "I think she's gained weight."

Gramp winked. "Good sign for an elephant!"

"We got the new camels," Jesse piped up. "At first they didn't like Pegleg, but he made friends with them."

"Where is Pegleg?" Gramp asked, looking around. "Hey, Pegleg!" At the sound of his name, Pegleg hopped over. "That's a good boy," Gramp said, scratching the little dog's head.

Finally, Gramp turned to Arden. "How are you, Missy? And how's Glory?"

"She's great," said Arden. "We're both really excited about the race!"

"So am I!" Gramp said. "I told those

darned doctors they'd better let me out of that hospital because my granddaughter was about to win a race and I couldn't miss it!"

"Now don't start complaining about your doctors," Gran said. "They did a pretty good job on you."

"I suppose so," Gramp admitted. Then he took in a big breath of air and smiled. "Sure is good to be home, though!" he said. "It even smells good!"

"Wait till you get a whiff of those new camels," Tim giggled.

"Let's go take a look at them now," said Gramp.

"Then let's go over to the bird sanctuary!" suggested Jesse.

"And after that Gramp can watch me take out Glory!" said Arden.

"Hold on, kids!" Gran warned. "Your Gramp may be out of the hospital, but he's not a hundred percent yet. He still has to take it easy for a while."

"Nonsense!" Thomas Quinn protested. He put an arm around Tansy.

"You worry too much," he said gently.

Arden smiled at her grandparents. It was so good to have Gramp back!

The whole family was about to go inside when they heard a car turn into the driveway. A shiny silver Cadillac was heading toward them.

"Company already?" Gramp smiled.

"I don't recognize that car," Gran said, "but I'm sure whoever's driving it is worth a pitcher of lemonade."

Leaving Gramp with a pat on the back, Gran went into the house. Arden, Jesse, and Tim stood clear of the driveway as the car came to a stop. Arden's heart did a funny flip-flop when she caught sight of the driver. It was Sam Silver — the Kentucky horse breeder. As usual he was wearing his derby.

"Howdy!" Mr. Silver called, climbing out of the car.

"What can I do for you?" Gramp asked warmly.

Silver tipped his hat to Arden and gave her a smile. "Young lady. . . ."

"Hi," Arden mumbled.

"I don't think I've had the pleasure," Gramp said.

Silver held out his hand. "Sam Silver," he introduced himself. "I'm a friend of Jed Wentworth's."

Gramp shook Mr. Silver's hand. "Any friend of Jed's is a friend of mine!" he said.

Just then Gran called the kids inside for something to eat. Jesse and Tim made a beeline for the house, but Arden stayed put. She wanted to know just what Sam Silver was doing here!

"Jed told me about your farm," Silver explained to Gramp. "Is that Glory out there with the elephant? I hope she isn't in any danger."

"Oh, Glory and Thomasina are old friends," Gramp assured him.

"Don't mind my asking," Silver said apologetically. "It's just that I have a real soft spot for that little filly. I've been watching her at the track." He smiled at Arden again. "You're doing a

83

good job with her, young lady!"

Arden muttered a "Thank you" without returning the smile.

Silver turned toward the house as the back door opened and Gran came out. "Sorry I was so long!" she said, introducing herself to the guest. "Care to come in for a glass of lemonade?"

"No, thanks," the horse breeder replied. "I *would* like to go down and say hello to Glory, though. I want to get a better look at her before the race. As I said, I'm very interested in that horse."

Gramp lifted an eyebrow. "I see. I didn't know Jed was planning to sell Glory."

Silver grinned. "You never know," he said. "I'm always looking to buy a winner."

"I'm pleased you think the horse's chances are good," said Gramp, giving Arden a nod.

"I think they're better than good," said Silver. "You know," he went on, "I bought the colt that came in first at

Wentworth last year. Might be worth my while to buy this year's winner, too!"

"Well, I'll be glad to show you Glory," Gramp said agreeably, "as long as Jed Wentworth says it's all right."

"It's not all right!" Arden blurted out. "Glory's resting!" She turned to Sam Silver. "No one should go down there! Leave her alone!"

"Arden!" Gran chided. "That's no way to speak to a guest! Mr. Silver only wants to look at Glory!"

Gramp sized up the situation. "Maybe Arden could use a nice, cool glass of lemonade," he suggested kindly.

"Yes, why don't you go inside and get some?" Gran said in a softer tone. "I made some sandwiches, too. And there's a letter from your mom and dad inside my satchel."

Arden's eyes flew open. "A letter? From Mom and Dad?"

"That's right," Gran said, smiling. "It's a big fat envelope, right in the side pocket of my — "

But Arden was already tearing off to the kitchen. She couldn't believe the letter had finally come!

"It's here! It's here!" she cried, bursting in through the back door. Jesse and Tim were sitting at the kitchen table. "The money from Mom and Dad is in Gran's satchel!"

Tim grabbed the satchel from the sideboard. Arden and Jesse crowded around him as he rummaged through the bag and came up with a bulky envelope addressed in their mother's handwriting.

"I've got it!" Tim said. "Look how thick it is!"

"They must have sent the money in dollar bills," said Jesse.

"It came just in time!" Arden exclaimed. "What a neat welcome home surprise for Gramp!"

The envelope was heavily taped, and Tim tugged at it furiously. "Look at all this stuff," he muttered. "I guess they didn't want the money to get lost in the mail."

"Hurry up and open it," Jesse said impatiently.

Tim opened the envelope with a rip, spilling some of the contents onto the floor and under the table.

"You dropped it!" Jesse cried. In a flash he was down on his hands and knees.

Meanwhile, Tim was dumping the packet out on the table.

"Wait a minute!" he cried in alarm. "What's this . . . ? There isn't any money here. It's only a bunch of pictures!"

"That's all these are, too!" Jesse exclaimed, picking some photographs off the floor.

"Maybe they sent a check," Arden said anxiously.

Tim shuffled through the stack of pictures and shook out the envelope. A single sheet of paper floated down to the floor. Arden scurried to pick it up. "It's not a check," she said. "It's only a letter."

"What does it say?" Jesse asked.

"Let me see it," said Tim.

Arden handed Tim the letter and he read it out loud.

" 'Dear Tim, Arden, and Jesse, Here are some pictures of Kilimanjaro. We left Nairobi a little earlier than planned. The wildlife is wonderful here! We miss you. Love, Dad and Mom.' "

"Kiliman . . . manjaro," Jesse moaned, not even sure how to pronounce it. "Where's that?"

"It's another place in Africa," Tim said grimly. "Mom and Dad were going there after they left Nairobi."

"But where's the money?" Jesse said, "Why didn't they send it?"

"They must not have gotten our telegram," Arden replied sadly.

Jesse started to cry. "Now we'll have to tell Gramp and Gran!"

Arden put a comforting arm around her little brother's shoulder.

"That's all Gramp needs to hear on his first day out of the hospital!" Tim sighed, kicking a chair in frustration.

"Let's not tell them yet," said Arden. "Let's wait until — "

"After the race?" Tim finished.

Arden nodded. "That way, if Glory wins and I get the thousand dollars, at least they'll have half of what they need!"

"And then we can all figure out how to get the rest," Tim said, brightening. "Don't cry, Jess! Everything's going to be all right!"

Arden's pulse began to pound. Now that the money hadn't come from Mom and Dad, winning the race was more important than ever! It was their only hope of saving River Oaks. She and Glory just *had* to do it!

Arden walked over to the window and looked outside. A smile flashed across her face as she caught sight of Glory down in the meadow. But it faded fast. There, standing right next to Glory, was the man in the derby hat — Sam Silver.

Chapter Nine

——◆——

A Matter of Honor

Arden and Glory sprinted around the Wentworth track. It was one of the filly's last practice runs and Arden could tell it was going to be good. The hot wind whipped her face as she led Glory through her paces. With perfect control, they rounded the track at lightning speed. Clocking the horse at the sideline were Jed Wentworth and Joey.

"Best ever!" Joey shouted as Arden streaked past him.

"Nothing short of a miracle," Wentworth said, looking at his stopwatch.

Arden trotted back quickly. Her face

was flushed from the workout, and Glory's mane dripped with perspiration. "How did we do?" she asked.

"Just a second over the record for this track," Wentworth announced.

"Fantastic!" yelled Arden. Glory snorted with excitement. "I knew we could do it!"

"This makes Glory and Winsome the two favored mounts," Wentworth added, turning to Joey. "Congratulations. You've trained the horse well."

"It helps to have a good jockey like Arden," Joey said proudly.

Beaming, Arden leaned over and hugged the filly's neck. "Good work, Glory!" she whispered.

"I'm proud of you, too, Arden," Mr. Wentworth said, looking up at her. "You've worked hard. You'll deserve that thousand-dollar prize if you're the winning rider. You'll deserve a lot more."

"Thanks, Mr. Wentworth," said Arden. "I'm going to do my very best."

Wentworth looked her straight in the

eye. "I know you will. And another thing," he added. "I never believed that story Miss Van Vreen cooked up after Winsome threw her. You're a good sport all the way. I know you'd never try to bump a rider."

"Thank you, Mr. Wentworth," Arden said gratefully.

"Why don't you go cool down now," Joey instructed. "I'll meet you later."

Knowing Mr. Wentworth didn't believe she'd been guilty of misconduct meant a lot to Arden, and she gave the two men a happy wave before she and Glory trotted off to the stable.

After removing Glory's saddle and bridle, Arden hosed the horse down. Glory whinnied as the cool stream of water hit her body. Then Arden dried the animal with a towel. She was just checking Glory's hooves when Tiffany walked over.

"What do you want?" Arden asked, looking up.

"I didn't mean to get in the way,"

Tiffany answered with a rare smile.

Arden went back to examining Glory's feet.

"Glory's a good horse," Tiffany said, leaning back on the fence. "I hear Sam Silver wants to buy her."

Arden flinched. "He did say something about buying the winner," she admitted.

"Even if Winsome came in first, I wouldn't dream of selling him," said Tiffany. "But if Glory won, I bet you Mr. Wentworth would sell her in a minute."

"Why do you think he'd do that?" Arden challenged.

"For the money, of course," said Tiffany.

Arden eyed Tiffany suspiciously. The girl was such a liar, Arden didn't know whether to believe her or not. She stood up and began to check Glory's ears.

"Did I tell you my aunt gave me money to buy another horse?" Tiffany boasted. "Two thousand dollars! If you had that much you could buy a horse, too."

"I don't need another horse," Arden said, "I have Glory."

"But Glory isn't even yours," Tiffany needled. "Of course, if you had two thousand dollars like I do, you could buy her yourself."

Arden sighed. "If only I did have two thousand dollars," she thought out loud.

"Come on," goaded Tiffany. "If you did have the money, what would you do with it?"

"I . . . I'd do something important for my grandparents," Arden said quietly before turning away from Tiffany and leading Glory into the stable.

Tiffany's eyes lit up. "I know what you're talking about!" she exclaimed, following Arden inside. "You're talking about that money your grandfather owes the bank, aren't you?"

Arden spun around. "How do you

know about that?" she asked furiously.

Tiffany shrugged. "My aunt is friends with the bank president. He was over at dinner the other night, talking about how your grandparents were going to lose River Oaks. Your grandfather doesn't know how to manage his money."

Arden felt like strangling Tiffany. "Don't you dare talk that way about my grandfather!" she warned her.

"Take it easy," Tiffany said. "I just think it's funny that you'd give the money to your grandfather. I'd spend it on myself."

Arden led Glory to her stall and tried to collect herself. With shaking hands she put fresh hay into the horse's feeder. Then she took a deep breath. "River Oaks is a very important place," Arden struggled to explain to Tiffany. "We have to save it."

Seating herself on a hay bale, Tiffany said, "*I* know how you can get the money for your grandfather."

"I'm going to try to get some of it by winning this race," Arden said, sticking her chin out.

"But the rider gets only one thousand dollars," Tiffany exclaimed. "You need two thousand. If you'll just listen to me, I'll tell you how you can get it all."

Arden drew closer. "What are you talking about?" she asked curiously.

Tiffany's blue eyes narrowed as she leaned toward Arden. "It's simple," she whispered. "All you have to do is let me win the race."

Arden looked confused. "What? How can I do that?"

"Easy," Tiffany said, smiling. "Winsome and Glory are the two top horses. Winsome's a sure thing if Glory drops out."

"But Glory can't drop out of the race," Arden exclaimed. "Mr. Wentworth wants her to run and — "

"Don't be such a baby," Tiffany said impatiently. She glanced over her shoulder to make sure no one else was listen-

ing. "You and Glory would still run in
the race. All you'd have to do is let me
and Winsome come in first. Hold Glory
back a little just before she gets to the
finish."

Arden was shocked. "But that's
cheating!" she protested. "I would never
do that — not for anything!"

97

"Not even for two thousand dollars?" Tiffany said slyly.

Arden's head began to spin. "I — I couldn't," she stammered.

"Why not?" challenged Tiffany. "All your problems would be over. You could give your grandfather the money he needs. Remember, even if you *are* the winning rider, you'll only get one thousand dollars. But your grandfather needs *two* thousand."

Arden shook her head vigorously. "I couldn't do that. It would be wrong!"

"But no one would know, " Tiffany argued. "Besides," she added, "if you try as hard as you can and Glory *does* win, Mr. Wentworth will sell her to Sam Silver. Then you'll never see Glory again in your whole life."

Arden looked at Glory and a pang went through her. The thought of losing Glory was almost unbearable. But still. . . .

"How do I know you're telling the truth?" Arden asked. "You lied about the day you fell on the track."

Tiffany shrugged. "Oh, that! Did you really expect me to tell the truth and get suspended? Winning this race is more important to me than anything. My aunt *expects* me to win."

"It's important to me, too!" said Arden.

"Don't be silly!" said Tiffany. "It would be better for you to lose. Then you'd have everything you want. Glory could stay at River Oaks and you could help your grandparents."

"Do you really have two thousand dollars?" Arden asked hesitantly.

"I've got my own bank account," Tiffany answered. "My aunt says I can do what I like with it."

Arden turned away. What Tiffany was suggesting seemed terrible, and yet. . . .

"Think about it," Tiffany said, giving Arden a pat on the shoulder. "But be sure to give me your answer before the race." And with a toss of her long, blonde curls, she walked out of the stable.

Arden was left alone in Glory's stall, bewildered. She had never cheated in her life, but Tiffany made it sound almost like a good thing. "What do *you* think I should do, Glory?" she whispered, stroking the horse's velvety-soft nose. "If only you could tell me."

Chapter Ten

Win or Lose

"It's a big day, girl," Arden crooned, leading Glory into her stall at Wentworth. The stable was already filling up as the other young jockeys arrived with their horses.

Glory had been fed and warmed up before they left River Oaks. All Arden had to do now was groom her and put on the racing saddle. As she ran the brush along Glory's flanks, the filly trembled and pawed the earth. "Calm down, girl," Arden coaxed. "We've still got a few minutes before the race begins."

Arden looked up as Joey came into the stall. "All set?" he asked.

Arden nodded and picked up the lavender saddle blanket with the big number 3 stitched in gold. Her hands shook as she laid it over Glory's back.

"Nervous?" Joey asked.

"A little bit," Arden admitted. "Glory's keyed up, too."

Joey smiled. "That's only natural. A bit of nerves can be a good thing. Gives you that extra boost you need to get over the finish line."

Arden turned to him. "Is it true that Mr. Silver bought the winner of the race last year?" she asked softly.

Joey nodded. "Yes, it is. But I don't want you worrying about that now." He tugged her ponytail playfully. "You just worry about winning!"

Arden looked up as Gramp and Gran rounded the corner with Jesse and Tim. "Just came to wish our favorite jockey good luck!" Gramp said proudly.

"We'll be rooting for you, darling!"

Gran said, giving Arden a kiss.

"We've got seats right down in the front!" Jesse chimed in.

Suddenly Arden felt like crying. Tim and Jesse and Gran and Gramp and Joey believed in her so much. They would all be out there cheering! They wanted her and Glory to win! But they had no idea what was really at stake. If Arden won this race she'd be losing more than she could bear — the chance to save River Oaks, and the horse she loved so dearly.

"We'll scoot now," Gran said, giving Arden another kiss.

Tim gave her a hug. "Good luck, sis!" he whispered. "You're doing this for all of us!"

Arden hugged Tim back. How she longed to blurt out everything — to tell Tim Tiffany's whole plan. But she couldn't. And if she deliberately lost the race, she could never tell anyone!

After the family left, Arden and Joey gave Glory a last-minute check. Then Arden put on her riding helmet.

Mr. Wentworth was waiting for them when Arden walked Glory out into the paddock. "She looks great!" he said approvingly. "How was her workout this morning?"

"Good as ever," replied Joey.

Arden climbed up into the saddle. "Thanks for everything, Arden!" said Mr. Wentworth. "Whatever happens in the race, you'll always be a winner in my book!"

Arden avoided his eyes. If she lost the race on purpose, Mr. Wentworth would be the main person she was cheating! "Thank you for letting me ride Glory," she said weakly. "I love her . . . almost like she was my own."

The stable owner started to say something in reply, but he was cut off by an official announcement blaring over the loudspeaker. It was time for all mounts and their riders to join the procession from the paddock to the gate.

"Good luck!" Joey said, reaching up to squeeze Arden's hand.

"See you later!" said Mr. Wentworth. "In the winner's circle," he added with a smile.

And then Arden and Glory moved out.

A wave of excitement rippled through the grandstand as the lean, spirited thoroughbreds gathered for the procession. Born to run, the horses snorted joyfully. The young jockeys were excited, too. Dressed in the bright colors of their stables, the boys and girls glanced around in tense anticipation. Arden spotted Tiffany on Winsome. The girl was wearing the emerald-green of Terrabella. Arden patted her own lavender and gold silks — Wentworth's colors.

"I've been waiting for a chance to talk," Tiffany whispered, sidling up to Arden. "Have you made up your mind, yet?"

"I'm not sure," Arden choked. Beads of sweat broke out on her forehead. She had so much to gain if she went along with Tiffany's plan, but now, when it came to actually committing herself to it. . . .

"If Glory wins, Mr. Wentworth will sell her to Sam Silver!" Tiffany warned urgently.

"I know," Arden moaned.

Tiffany's hard, blue eyes bored through her. "And what about River Oaks and your grandparents? I thought you wanted to help them."

Arden tried to think clearly, but her mind was a blur. A second announcement came over the loudspeaker: "All riders proceed to the gate!"

"What's it going to be?" Tiffany hissed.

"I . . . I . . . I'll do it your way," Arden faltered.

As Tiffany smiled triumphantly and bounded off for the start, a wave of shame washed over Arden.

What have I done? she thought. Not once in her whole life had Arden Quinn cheated at anything. Her parents had taught her that it was wrong! She knew it was wrong. And yet she'd just agreed to lose the race to Tiffany.

Glancing off into the crowd of spectators, Arden caught sight of Gramp, Gran, and her brothers. I can't do this to them, she told herself. But then she caught sight of Sam Silver in a special box. It's not really cheating! Arden wavered. And it's for such a good cause!

Arden tried to hold her head high as Glory trotted proudly toward the gate. Jesse and Tim waved from the grandstand.

Entering the chute, Glory became restless. "It's all right, girl," Arden whispered soothingly. "We've practiced this before. Remember?"

Glory stood obediently, with her nose up. But Arden could feel the anticipation in the filly's powerful body. Like an arrow about to be let loose from a tautly drawn bow, Glory was ready. Arden's body tingled with anticipation, too. Straight ahead was the oval track she'd learned to love. She quickly went over the race in her mind: the first turn, backstretch, final turn, then home to the finish! She'd run it a hundred times.

For the moment, Tiffany and the problems at River Oaks were forgotten. There was nothing on Arden's mind but the race. She and Glory had worked so hard for this moment. . . .

The starting bell rang — and off they ran! Glory surged through the gate, and in a single instant she took the lead. The official's voice boomed over the loudspeaker: "And out in front — it's Rappadan Glory!"

Wind whipped at Arden's face as Glory thundered down the track.

At the first turn, the loudspeaker blared again: "And still out front — it's Rappadan Glory!"

Arden leaned forward and felt the charge of the filly's electrifying energy as she galloped down the backstretch. Out of the corner of her eye, Arden saw Tiffany and Winsome gaining.

"What are you doing?" Tiffany

snarled, coming up next to her. "Get out of my way!"

The announcer's voice rang out once more: "Neck and neck before the final turn, it's Winsome and Glory!"

Arden couldn't tell which was pounding louder — the horses' hooves or her own heart. This was it! If she was going to let up, she'd have to do it now! But as Arden felt Glory strain to regain the lead, she hesitated for a split second. Glory was born to race — born to win. How could Arden deny her this victory?

The final turn loomed ahead. Suddenly Arden thought of Mr. Wentworth and how he trusted her. She remembered the day she'd been accused of misconduct. "You're Arden Quinn!" she heard Gran's voice saying. "You've got too much of that Quinn honor to ever cheat!"

With all her strength, Arden pressed her knees against Glory's body. She just couldn't do it! "Sorry!" she gasped, glancing over at Tiffany. "I can't. . . ."

The words were carried off by the wind, as Glory flew past Winsome.

The announcer's voice rang out: "And at the final turn, it's still Rappadan Glory!"

But starting down the homestretch, Winsome came up again. The two horses were nose to nose. Tiffany was screaming and using her whip. And then, "It's Winsome!" the announcer's voice sang out. "It's Winsome out front, followed by Rappadan Glory!"

Tears flew from the corners of Arden's eyes as she and Glory strained to take the lead again. She gave Glory her head and the filly bounded forward. The finish line seemed to be flying toward them.

"And out front again — Rappadan Glory!" The announcer's voice could barely be heard over the roar of the crowd.

"Go, Glory! Go!" Arden cried. The filly's hooves left the ground, and then they sailed across the finish! Arden's heart felt as it if would burst!

A final announcement echoed over the loudspeaker: "And the winner! — Rappadan Glory, owned by Jed Wentworth. The rider, Miss Arden Quinn of River Oaks!"

As Arden dismounted, she was suddenly surrounded by fans and photographers. Joey ran over and grabbed her hand. "You did it!" he cried.

Arden could hardly catch her breath. She looked up and saw her brothers pushing their way through the crowd. "Tim!" she cried. "Jesse!"

"Here we are, Arden!" Tim answered, engulfing her in a bear hug. "You were great!"

"You won! You won!" Jesse shouted, jumping up and down in excitement.

Close by, Gramp beamed proudly at his granddaughter, while Gran dabbed her eyes with a handkerchief. Mr. Wentworth stepped in to pose with Arden and Glory for the photographers. "Your picture's going to be in the paper!" he told Arden with a wink. "Hope that doesn't bother you!"

"It's great," Arden said. She looked into Mr. Wentworth's pale blue eyes. "Glory ran a good race. Thanks for letting me be her jockey. It was a real honor."

Wentworth patted her hand. "The honor was mine," he replied warmly. Tears welled up in Arden's eyes. To think that she'd been about to give up her honor. She was so glad she'd changed her mind and hadn't cheated!

"Well, what's next, Mr. Wentworth?" Joey asked, patting Glory enthusiastically. "Are you going to send this filly to Kentucky to win the Derby?"

Arden's heart skipped a beat. She had almost forgotten about Sam Silver.

"The Derby, huh?" Wentworth chuckled. "Well, who knows? Maybe Glory will make it there someday. It's sure in her bloodline. But that's a decision her new owner will have to make."

Arden gulped and glanced out into the crowd for Sam Silver. The horse breeder was still in his box, observing the festivities.

"You're going to sell Glory?" Arden said anxiously.

"Not exactly," Wentworth said. And when Arden gave him a puzzled look, he reached into the pocket of his white suit, pulled out an envelope, and handed it to her. "Here," he said gruffly. "Read this."

"These are Glory's papers," Arden said, bewildered.

Wentworth winked. "Keep them in a safe place, now!"

"But . . . but why do you want *me* to keep them?" Arden stammered, not understanding. She looked at Gramp and Gran and Joey. They were all smiling as if they shared some secret.

Jed Wentworth laughed. "I told you Glory was getting a new owner, didn't I?"

Arden nodded.

He clasped Arden's hand. "Well, she is. The new owner is *you!*"

Arden gasped, hardly daring to believe her ears. "You mean, you're giving Glory to *me?!*"

"That's exactly what I mean," Wentworth said. "You have a real gift with this horse. And for taking such good care of her, these ownership papers are my gift to you!"

"Forever?" Arden asked.

Wentworth nodded. "Forever! I signed her over to you even before the race. Win or lose, I wanted you to have your dream come true!"

"Did you hear that, Gramp?" Arden exclaimed. "Gran! Glory's mine!"

Gran smiled and squeezed Arden's arm. "We know, darling! It's wonderful!"

"I can't believe it!" Arden said, beaming at Mr. Wentworth. "I was so sure you were going to sell her to Sam Silver!"

"Silver did say he might be interested in Glory, especially if she did well in the race," Wentworth admitted. "But I told him early on that I had other plans for this filly."

"But he was going to give you a lot of money," Arden persisted. "Wasn't he?"

Wentworth waved his hand good-naturedly. "There are still a few things that are worth more than the almighty dollar!"

"Speaking of the almighty dollar," Joey cracked, "as of today, Miss Arden Quinn is quite a rich young lady!"

"That's right!" Tim said gleefully. "Arden won a thousand dollars!"

"She won more than that!" said Jed Wentworth. "As Glory's owner, she gets another thousand. So that means she's actually won two!"

"Oh, boy!" yelled Jesse. "Two thousand dollars. That's just what we need. Oops!" he added, feeling Tim's elbow in his ribs. "I mean, that's great, Arden!"

Tim pulled the younger boy aside. "Can't we tell Gran and Gramp yet?"

whispered Jesse. "Now that we've got the money!"

"Not yet!" Tim said. "I think Arden should do it!"

But Arden was so overcome with emotion she could hardly speak. Tears streamed down her face as she stroked Glory's mane.

"*Now* can we tell Gran and Gramp?" Jesse wheedled.

"Not yet!" Tim hissed. "Arden wants to wait until the cake!"

"What are you two boys whispering about over there?" Gran asked. She was standing at the counter, taking the cover off a big cake box. Arden, looking tired but happy, was seated in the place of honor at the head of the table.

"More milk, anybody?" Gramp called from the refrigerator.

"I'll have some!" Joey answered. "That was a mighty fine meal, Mrs. Quinn," he complimented Gran.

Gramp brought over the milk while

Gran set down a luscious chocolate cake
decorated with lavender roses. The name
Arden was spelled out in lavender letters.

"I wish Glory could have some of
this," Arden said. "It's really beautiful,
Gran. Thank you!"

"Gramp and I had an idea we'd be celebrating tonight," Gran said, smiling.

"So what are you going to do with all that money you won?" Joey asked, sneaking some icing off the cake plate.

Arden looked at Tim and Jesse, then turned back to her grandparents. "I'm going to give it to River Oaks," she said quietly.

"I don't understand," Gramp said. "That money belongs to you, Arden."

"But River Oaks needs it for the mortgage," Jesse blurted out.

"That's right," Tim said. "We saw the letter from the bank, and — "

"Hold on a minute," Gramp interrupted. "Suppose you start from the beginning."

Gran and Gramp and Joey listened in amazement as Tim told how they'd opened the letter from the bank and then tried to think of ways to get the money.

"You children!" Gran scolded gently. "Gramp and I don't need your money. I simply forgot to make a payment."

"So that's what happened to the bank's reminder to us," Gramp said, a bit more severely. "You shouldn't have kept the letter from your grandmother," he went on. "You can't imagine how surprised we were when the bank called yesterday to ask about our payment."

"But now we have the money," Jesse said eagerly.

"That's right," said Arden. "I want you and Gran to use the prize money for River Oaks. I was thinking about how I'd help you all while I was training for the race. That's one reason it was so important!"

Gramp sighed and smiled. "You make me so proud," he said, "all three of you."

"We can't let you pay our debts," Gran put in.

"You can't let the bank close River Oaks!" Tim exclaimed.

"No, you can't!" Arden pleaded.

"Hush now, everybody!" Gramp smiled. "Who said anything about closing River Oaks? I paid the bill this morning. The check's already in the mail and the bank's expecting it."

"But it was so much money," Tim said. "We thought — "

"I'll admit we've had some rough moments here at River Oaks," Gramp said, looking around the table. "But your Gran and I have always gotten through them somehow. This time it was Miner's Pretzels that saved the day."

Arden looked puzzled. "Miner's Pretzels?"

Gramp smiled. "A big check came in for Mortie's commercial. In fact, it's giving your Gran and me some ideas about how to raise money for the farm in the future."

"Well, I'll be!" chuckled Joey. "Put the animals to work in show business, huh? Let them pay their own way!"

"We think it's a possibility," Gran said. "Of course we'll have to find out exactly how to go about it. Mortie's commercial was just a fluke — pure luck."

Tim's eyes lit up and he turned to Arden. "Wow, sis! If Gran and Gramp don't need the money, it means you really are rich!"

"Yeah!" said Jesse. "You've got two thousand whole dollars! I wonder if Mr. Wentworth will give it to you in dollar bills!"

"I'm sure Mr. Wentworth will be sending a check," Gramp chuckled. "And I think what we'll do is open a bank account for your sister. Don't you think that would be nice, Arden?"

"I guess so," said Arden, not knowing what to make of this turn of events.

"That's a very good idea," Gran agreed. "We'll start a fund for college." She handed Arden a cake knife. "And now will you please serve the cake for us, Arden?"

Arden smiled as she cut into the rich chocolate cake.

"Maybe you'd like to spend that two thousand dollars on oats for Glory," Joey teased, passing his plate over.

"If I had two thousand dollars, I'd buy a bunch of mynah birds!" said Jesse. "And some more dogs."

"I'd buy an elephant like Thomasina," said Tim.

"You'd better buy a big piece of land to put her on," Gramp warned.

"That's a good idea," said Arden eagerly. If she saved all the money she made until she grew up, she and Jesse and Tim could buy their very own animal rescue farm — just like River Oaks! There would be birds and big cats and elephants and lots of horses. . . .

Gran waved a hand in front of Arden's face. "Wake up, Arden. We're waiting for our cake."

"Sorry," Arden said. "I guess I was daydreaming."

"You must be tired," Gran said gently. "You've had a big day."

"Oh, she'll sleep tonight!" Gramp chuckled.

Arden could barely keep her eyes open long enough to finish her cake. But before heading off to bed, she went out to say good night to Glory.

"We've had some day, huh, girl?" she murmured, giving the horse a sugar cube.

As Arden leaned into Glory's dark neck and gave her a kiss, she wondered what the rest of their stay at River Oaks would be like. Maybe there'd be other races for her and Glory. Maybe they'd win again, maybe they'd lose. But Arden knew one thing for sure: Whatever happened, she and Glory would always give it their best shot! She and Glory would always be together!